CU00955571

# Cont

## Chapter 7: The Danger Lurking

- Discover a new predator that poses a threat to the ant and its colony
- Learn about the importance of being aware of potential dangers

## Chapter 8: The Search for Help

- Venture out to find allies to help protect the colony
- Meet new insect friends and convince them to help

## Chapter 9: The Battle Plan

- Work together to come up with a plan to defeat the predator
- Learn about the importance of strategy and planning

## Chapter 10: The Epic Battle

- Fight against the predator with the help of newfound allies
- Experience the excitement and suspense of the battle

## Chapter 11: The Victory

- Celebrate the victory over the predator and the safety of the colony
- Learn about the importance of standing up to bullies and protecting what is important

## Chapter 12: The New Adventure

- Discover a new mission for the ant and its colony
- Continue to explore the wonders of the natural world

## Chapter 13: The Friendship

- Meet a new insect friend who is different from the ant in many ways
- Learn about the value of accepting and appreciating differences

## Chapter 14: The Learning Journey

- Explore new territories and discover new things about the world
- Learn about different types of plants, animals and insects

## Chapter 15: The Self-Discovery

- Encounter challenges that test the ant's strengths and weaknesses
- Learn about self-discovery and the importance of knowing oneself

## Chapter 16: The Problem-Solving

- Face a problem that requires creative thinking and problem-solving skills
- Work with other insects to come up with a solution

## Chapter 17: The Importance of Rest

- Learn about the importance of taking breaks and resting
- Discover how rest and relaxation can help increase productivity

## Chapter 18: The Homecoming

- Return to the ant's nest and share the knowledge and experiences gained
- Celebrate the growth and achievements of the ant and its colony

## Chapter 19: The Mystery of the Missing Ants

- Investigate the disappearance of some of the ant's friends
- Search for clues and work to solve the mystery

## Chapter 20: The Unexpected Alliance

- Discover a new insect ally who has been affected by the same mystery
- Work together to uncover the truth and solve the mystery

## Chapter 21: The Truth Revealed

- Uncover the culprit behind the disappearance of the missing ants
- Learn about the consequences of one's actions and the importance of taking responsibility

## Chapter 22: The Rebuilding

- Help the colony recover and rebuild after the aftermath of the mystery
- Learn about the importance of resilience and moving forward

## Chapter 23: The Celebration

- Celebrate the reunion of the ant's friends and the success of the mystery-solving mission
- Learn about the importance of celebrating accomplishments and milestones

## Chapter 24: The New Horizon

- Look to the future and plan for new adventures and missions
- Learn about the endless possibilities and opportunities that lie ahead.

## Chapter 25: The Great Migration

- Follow the ant as it embarks on a great migration with its colony
- Discover the challenges and rewards of moving to a new location

## Chapter 26: The Adaptation

- **Le**arn how the ant and its colony adapt to the new environment
- Discover the importance of being able to adjust and adapt to change

## Chapter 27: The New Discoveries

- Explore the new environment and discover new things about the world
- Encounter new plants, animals and insects that the ant has never seen before

## Chapter 28: The Community

- Work together with other insects and animals to build a strong community
- Learn about the importance of cooperation and mutual support

## Chapter 29: The Natural Disaster

- Encounter a natural disaster, such as a flood or wildfire
- Learn about the impact of natural disasters on the environment and the importance of resilience

## Chapter 30: The Homecoming, Again

- Return to the ant's original nest and reflect on the incredible journey
- Celebrate the growth, resilience and achievements of the ant and its colony

## Epilogue: The Legacy

- Follow the ant's descendants as they continue to explore the world and face new challenges
- Reflect on the legacy and impact of the ant's incredible journey
- As the ant's story comes to a close, we see that its journey has had a lasting impact on its colony and on the world around it. The ant's bravery, resilience, and determination have inspired future generations of ants to explore, adapt, and thrive. We see the ant's descendants continuing the legacy of their ancestor, embarking on their own incredible journeys and discovering new wonders in the natural world.
- The epilogue serves as a reminder that our actions and adventures can have a lasting impact on those around us, and that we can all leave a positive legacy through our courage, resilience, and determination. It also encourages readers to continue exploring the natural world, to embrace new challenges, and to never stop growing and learning.

# Summary

"The Incredible Journey of the Tiny Ant" is a story about a brave and determined ant who embarks on a journey to find food for her colony. Along the way, she faces many obstacles and challenges, but with the help of her friends, she overcomes them all. Through their journey, the ants learn the importance of teamwork, problem-solving, and perseverance. The story also highlights the themes of friendship, self-discovery, and the power of community. Ultimately, the ants realize that their legacy will live on through the lessons they have learned and the values they have instilled in future generations.

# *Chapter 1: The Departure*

Once upon a time, in a bustling ant colony deep in the forest, there lived a tiny ant named Alvin. Alvin had always been fascinated by the world beyond the colony's borders, and dreamed of one day venturing out into the unknown.

As the summer drew to a close and the leaves began to turn golden, Alvin noticed a restlessness in the colony. The ants were busy scurrying to and fro, carrying food and supplies, and chattering excitedly among themselves. Alvin sensed that something important was happening.

One day, as he was wandering through the colony, Alvin heard a rhythmic tapping sound. It was coming from the center of the colony, where the queen and her council of elders held court.

Curious, Alvin followed the sound and peered through a gap in the leaves. He saw a group of ants gathered around the queen, tapping their feet in time to a strange and captivating rhythm.

Alvin was entranced. He had never heard anything like this before. The rhythm seemed to echo the beating of his own heart, and he felt an inexplicable urge to move to the beat.

Before he knew it, Alvin had joined the crowd of ants, tapping his own feet and swaying to the rhythm. The queen smiled down at him and nodded her approval. Alvin felt a surge of pride and excitement. It seemed that he had been chosen for something special.

As the rhythmic tapping continued, Alvin realized that it was a signal. The colony was preparing for departure - they were about to embark on a great journey into the unknown.

Alvin's heart raced with excitement. This was the moment he had been waiting for. He was about to leave the safety and comfort of his home, and set out on an incredible journey of discovery.

As the rhythm reached its climax, Alvin took a deep breath, and stepped forward to join the column of ants marching towards the colony's exit. The journey had begun.

As Alvin followed the column of ants, he couldn't help but feel a sense of trepidation mixed with excitement. The world outside the colony was vast and unknown, filled with both wonders and dangers. But he was determined to explore it all and bring back new discoveries to his colony.

The sound of the rhythmic tapping continued to fill the air as the ants marched forward. Alvin found himself tapping his feet and swaying to the beat once again, feeling a sense of unity and purpose with his fellow ants.

As they reached the entrance of the colony, the bright light of the outside world flooded in. Alvin shielded his eyes and stepped forward, ready to face whatever lay ahead. The journey of a lifetime had begun.

# Chapter 2: The Obstacle Course

Alvin and his fellow ants marched forward, their tiny feet tapping out a steady rhythm on the forest floor. The sun beat down on them, casting long shadows across the forest floor.

As they traveled deeper into the forest, Alvin began to notice the terrain changing. The ground grew rougher, and the air grew thicker with the scent of damp earth and decaying leaves.

Suddenly, the rhythmic tapping stopped. Alvin looked around, confused, and saw that the path ahead was blocked by a massive obstacle course.

The course was made up of a series of towering obstacles, including steep inclines, slippery slides, and narrow ropes to balance on. Alvin's heart sank as he realized that he would have to navigate through it all in order to continue on the journey.

But he wasn't alone. Alvin's fellow ants quickly sprang into action, splitting up into teams and tackling the obstacles one by one. They worked together, using their strength, agility, and determination to overcome each challenge.

Alvin watched in awe as the ants bravely climbed the steep inclines and slid down the slippery slopes. He felt a sense of camaraderie and belonging with his fellow ants, and knew that together, they could overcome anything.

Finally, it was Alvin's turn to face the obstacle course. His heart raced as he approached the first challenge - a narrow rope bridge suspended high above a deep ravine.

Alvin took a deep breath and stepped onto the rope. He wobbled unsteadily at first, but soon found his balance and began to make his way across. The wind buffeted him from side to side, but he kept his eyes focused on the end of the bridge.

With each obstacle that he overcame, Alvin felt a surge of confidence and pride. He realized that he was capable of much more than he had ever imagined, and that there was nothing he couldn't achieve with determination and courage.

As he crossed the final obstacle, a narrow beam high above the treetops, Alvin felt a rush of joy and triumph. He had faced his fears and overcome the obstacle course, and he knew that he was ready for whatever challenges lay ahead.

# Chapter 3: The Teamwork

After successfully navigating the obstacle course, Alvin and his fellow ants continued on their journey, their tiny feet tapping out a steady rhythm on the forest floor.

As they marched on, Alvin noticed that the path ahead grew steeper and more treacherous. The ants began to slow down, their rhythmic tapping faltering as they struggled to keep pace.

Alvin realized that they were faced with a new challenge, one that could not be overcome through sheer strength and determination alone. They would need to work together, using their individual strengths to support one another and overcome the obstacle ahead.

Alvin stepped forward, his heart racing with excitement and determination. He knew that he had a role to play, and he was ready to do whatever it took to help his fellow ants.

As they approached the steep incline, Alvin noticed that some of the ants were struggling to climb it. He quickly sprang into action, using his small size and nimble feet to scurry up the incline and create a tiny ledge for the others to climb onto.

As the other ants climbed onto the ledge, Alvin watched in awe as they worked together to build a makeshift ladder, using their bodies to create a sturdy structure that would allow them to reach the top of the hill.

Despite the steep terrain and the hot sun beating down on them, the ants worked tirelessly, using their individual strengths to support one another and achieve their goal.

Finally, after hours of hard work, they reached the top of the hill. Alvin looked out over the stunning vista below, his heart swelling with pride and a sense of accomplishment.

He realized that the journey ahead would be filled with challenges and obstacles, but as long as they continued to work together and support one another, they could achieve anything. The rhythm of their tiny feet tapping in unison was a testament to the power of teamwork and the strength of unity.

# Chapter 4: The Unexpected Adventure rhythm story

Alvin and his fellow ants continued on their journey, their tiny feet tapping out a steady rhythm on the forest floor. As they marched on, the path ahead grew increasingly narrow and winding, until they found themselves standing at the edge of a deep, dark chasm.

Alvin peered down into the abyss, his heart racing with excitement and fear. He wondered what lay at the bottom, and if they would ever be able to make it across.

Suddenly, a gust of wind caught Alvin off guard, sending him tumbling over the edge and hurtling towards the darkness below.

As he fell, Alvin realized that he was not alone. His fellow ants were falling alongside him, their tiny bodies flailing wildly as they plummeted towards the unknown.

But just as suddenly as they had fallen, the ants were caught by a powerful updraft, which lifted them high into the air and sent them soaring over the chasm.

Alvin looked around in wonder, his tiny eyes wide with amazement. He realized that they were no longer on the forest floor, but were instead flying through the air on a magical journey.

As they soared over the treetops, Alvin and his fellow ants marveled at the stunning landscape below. They saw majestic mountains, shimmering lakes, and sprawling cities, all from a perspective that they had never before experienced.

Finally, after what felt like hours of flying, the ants began to descend back towards the forest floor. They landed softly on the ground, their tiny feet tapping out a rhythm of awe and wonder.

Alvin realized that their unexpected adventure had taught them a valuable lesson - that the world was full of surprises and that there was always something new to discover. The rhythm of their tiny feet tapping in gratitude and amazement was a testament to the limitless potential of exploration and the power of the unexpected.

# Chapter 5: The Final Hurdle

Alvin and his fellow ants continued on their journey, their tiny feet tapping out a steady rhythm on the forest floor. As they marched on, they found themselves facing their toughest challenge yet - a raging river that cut across their path.

The water was deep and swift, and the rocks were slippery and treacherous. Alvin knew that they would need to work together to cross the river and continue on their journey.

He gathered his fellow ants and began to devise a plan. They would create a raft using leaves and twigs, and use their tiny bodies to propel it across the water.

The ants worked tirelessly, gathering materials and constructing their raft with precision and care. Alvin took charge, directing his fellow ants to carefully stack the leaves and twigs to create a sturdy base for the raft.

Finally, after hours of hard work, the raft was complete. Alvin and his fellow ants climbed aboard, using their tiny feet to push the raft away from the shore and into the raging current.

The water was rough and the raft was small, but the ants were determined. They used their tiny bodies to paddle with all their might, their rhythmic tapping echoing across the water as they fought to reach the other side.

But just as they were about to make it to safety, disaster struck. A powerful current caught the raft, sending it tumbling downstream and throwing the ants into the water.

Alvin and his fellow ants fought to stay afloat, their tiny legs paddling frantically as they struggled to reach the shore. Finally, with a surge of determination, they managed to pull themselves onto dry land, exhausted and soaked to the bone.

As they collapsed onto the ground, panting and gasping for air, Alvin realized that they had accomplished their greatest challenge yet. They had worked together to overcome the final hurdle on their journey, and had emerged stronger and more resilient than ever before.

The rhythm of their tiny feet tapping in unison was a testament to the power of determination and perseverance in the face of adversity.

Alvin and his fellow ants had proven that anything was possible, as long as they worked together and kept the rhythm of their hearts beating as one.

# The Return

With the final hurdle conquered, Alvin and his fellow ants continued on their journey, their tiny feet tapping out a triumphant rhythm on the forest floor. They had come so far and had faced so many challenges, but they had never lost sight of their goal - to return home and share their amazing journey with their fellow ants.

As they marched on, they noticed that the forest around them had changed. The leaves had turned from vibrant greens to fiery oranges and deep reds, signaling the onset of autumn. The air was crisp and cool, and the ground was littered with fallen leaves.

Alvin and his fellow ants knew that they were getting closer to home. They could sense it in the rhythm of the forest, in the rustling of the leaves and the chirping of the birds.

Finally, after what felt like a lifetime of walking, Alvin and his fellow ants arrived at their home colony. They were greeted with cheers and applause from their fellow ants, who had been eagerly awaiting their return.

Alvin and his companions shared their incredible journey with their fellow ants, telling tales of their adventures and the many challenges they had faced and overcome. The other ants listened in awe, their tiny hearts beating in time with the rhythm of the story.

As the sun set on their amazing journey, Alvin and his fellow ants realized that they had been forever changed by their adventure. They had discovered the power of teamwork, the thrill of exploration, and the joy of discovering new things.

The rhythm of their tiny feet tapping in unison was a testament to the limitless potential of the human spirit, and to the boundless possibilities of the world around us. Alvin and his fellow ants knew that their journey had just begun, and that they would continue to explore and discover all that the world had to offer, one rhythmic step at a time.

# Chapter 7: The Danger Lurking

Alvin and his fellow ants had returned to their home colony, eager to rest and recover from their incredible journey. But as they settled back into their daily routine, they noticed something strange in the rhythm of the forest.

There was a new danger lurking, one that threatened to disrupt the delicate balance of their ecosystem. Alvin and his fellow ants could sense it in the rhythm of the leaves, in the scurrying of the insects, and in the way the air hung heavy with an eerie stillness.

They knew that they had to investigate, to discover the source of the danger and protect their colony from harm. So they set out, their tiny feet tapping out a steady rhythm as they ventured into the unknown.

As they journeyed deeper into the forest, they began to notice signs of the danger. Trees had been felled, animals had disappeared, and the ground was littered with strange debris.

Alvin and his fellow ants knew that they had to act fast. They gathered their forces and set about creating a plan to confront the danger head-on.

They worked tirelessly, tapping out their plan in rhythm as they constructed barriers and defenses, preparing for the worst. And when the danger finally arrived, they were ready.

A massive machine, manned by humans, had been cutting down the trees and disrupting the delicate balance of the forest. But Alvin and his fellow ants were not deterred. They swarmed the machine, their tiny bodies working in perfect rhythm as they worked to stop it in its tracks.

Their efforts were not in vain. The humans saw the error of their ways, and promised to work together with the ants to protect the forest and its inhabitants.

As the humans left, Alvin and his fellow ants settled back into their daily routine, their tiny feet tapping out a rhythm of victory and hope. They had faced a new danger and emerged victorious, proving once again the power of determination, teamwork, and the rhythm of the human spirit.

# Chapter 8: The Search for Help

The rhythm of the forest had changed once again, and this time it was not danger that was lurking, but illness. A strange sickness had descended upon the ants, causing them to weaken and falter in their daily routines.

Alvin and his fellow ants knew that they needed help, but they were not sure where to turn. So they set out on a new journey, their tiny feet tapping out a rhythm of urgency as they searched for someone who could heal them.

Their search took them far and wide, through fields of flowers and forests of towering trees. They met many creatures along the way, some friendly and some not, but none who could offer them the help they needed.

Finally, after what felt like an eternity of searching, Alvin and his fellow ants stumbled upon a wise old beetle who promised to help them in their time of need.

The beetle led them to a hidden grove, deep in the heart of the forest, where he brewed a magical potion from the nectar of rare flowers and the sap of ancient trees.

The ants drank the potion, and they felt their strength return. The rhythm of their tiny feet grew strong once more, and they knew that they had been healed.

They thanked the wise old beetle for his help, and set off back to their home colony, their tiny feet tapping out a rhythm of gratitude and joy.

As they journeyed back through the forest, they reflected on all that they had learned on their incredible journey. They had faced danger and illness, but they had also discovered the power of determination, the importance of teamwork, and the beauty of friendship.

And as they arrived back at their home colony, they knew that they were stronger and more united than ever before, their tiny feet tapping out a rhythm of hope for the future.

# Chapter 9: The Battle Plan

Alvin and his fellow ants had returned to their home colony, but they knew that they could not rest for long. A new danger was looming on the horizon, and they had to prepare themselves for battle.

The ants gathered together in a large group, tapping out a rhythm of determination as they discussed their options. They knew that they were facing a powerful enemy, and they had to come up with a plan that would give them the best chance of success.

As they talked, ideas began to form, and soon they had developed a battle plan that was both ingenious and effective. Their tiny feet tapped out a rhythm of excitement as they set to work, putting their plan into action.

They divided themselves into different groups, each with a specific task to perform. Some ants were tasked with gathering resources, while others were responsible for scouting out the enemy's movements. Still, others were assigned to create diversionary tactics and traps.

As the ants worked, their tiny feet tapped out a rhythm of precision and coordination. They moved with speed and purpose, each ant knowing exactly what they needed to do to bring their plan to fruition.

Finally, the day of the battle arrived. The ants approached the enemy with caution, tapping out a rhythm of wariness as they sized up their opponent. But they were not deterred. With a sudden surge of energy, the ants launched their attack, their tiny bodies moving in perfect rhythm as they executed their battle plan flawlessly.

The enemy was caught off guard, and they faltered under the force of the ants' attack. The ants fought with all their might, their tiny feet tapping out a rhythm of victory as they emerged triumphant.

As the enemy retreated, Alvin and his fellow ants knew that they had achieved something truly remarkable. They had faced a powerful adversary and emerged victorious, thanks to their determination, teamwork, and the rhythm of their movements.

As they returned to their home colony, their tiny feet tapping out a rhythm of pride, they knew that they had set an example for all the creatures of the forest. They had shown that even the smallest among us can achieve great things, as long as we work together and move in harmony with the rhythm of the world around us.

# Chapter 10: The Epic Battle

After their victory over the enemy, Alvin and his fellow ants thought that they could finally relax and enjoy the fruits of their labor. But they were wrong.

A new danger was approaching, and this one was even more formidable than the last. The ants could sense it in the air, a foreboding sense of impending doom that set their tiny bodies quivering.

As they gathered together, their tiny feet tapping out a rhythm of fear, they knew that they had to come up with a plan quickly. But what could they do against an enemy that was so powerful and so ruthless?

Alvin's mind raced as he thought about their options. They had to think outside the box, to come up with a strategy that was both unexpected and effective.

And then he had an idea.

It was a risky plan, one that could cost them dearly, but it was the only option they had left. Alvin shared his plan with the other ants, and they listened with rapt attention, their tiny feet tapping out a rhythm of determination.

They knew that this would be their toughest battle yet, but they were ready to face it head-on.

The day of the battle arrived, and the ants approached the enemy with a newfound confidence. Their tiny feet tapped out a rhythm of bravery as they surged forward, their numbers bolstered by an unlikely ally.

The battle was fierce and unforgiving. The ants fought with all their might, their tiny bodies moving in perfect rhythm as they dodged the enemy's attacks and struck back with deadly precision.

Their enemy was strong, but they were determined. Their tiny feet tapped out a rhythm of strength as they pushed forward, refusing to back down even in the face of overwhelming odds.

And then, just when it seemed like all was lost, they heard a familiar sound.

It was the rhythm of their allies, the insects and creatures of the forest who had been watching their battle from afar. Inspired by the ants' bravery and determination, they had decided to join the fight.

The ants and their allies fought side by side, their tiny feet tapping out a rhythm of unity and strength. Together, they overcame the enemy, their tiny bodies moving in perfect harmony as they emerged victorious.

As they stood on the battlefield, their tiny feet tapping out a rhythm of triumph, Alvin and his fellow ants knew that they had achieved something truly epic. They had faced their greatest challenge yet and emerged victorious, thanks to their bravery, determination, and the power of the rhythm that united them.

And as they returned to their home colony, their tiny feet tapping out a rhythm of pride and joy, they knew that they would never forget the lessons they had learned. They had shown that even the smallest among us can achieve great things when we work together and move in harmony with the rhythm of the world around us.

# Chapter 11: The Victory

As the ants returned to their home colony, they were greeted with cheers and celebration. Their tiny feet tapped out a rhythm of triumph as they shared the news of their victory over the enemy with their fellow ants.

The entire colony was in awe of what they had achieved, and they couldn't help but feel a sense of pride and gratitude for their brave comrades who had fought so fiercely on the battlefield.

But as the celebrations died down, Alvin and his fellow ants knew that they still had work to do. The aftermath of the battle had left them with many challenges to face, from rebuilding their colony to tending to the wounded.

Their tiny feet tapped out a rhythm of determination as they set to work, each ant doing their part to ensure that their home was once again safe and secure.

As they worked, they couldn't help but reflect on the lessons they had learned on their journey. They had discovered the power of teamwork, of working together and moving in harmony to achieve their goals.

They had also learned the importance of resilience and perseverance, of never giving up even in the face of overwhelming odds.

And most importantly, they had discovered the power of rhythm, of moving in harmony with the world around them to achieve greatness.

As they went about their tasks, their tiny feet tapping out a rhythm of purpose and determination, Alvin and his fellow ants knew that they were part of something bigger than themselves. They were part of a community that valued teamwork, resilience, and the power of rhythm.

And as they looked out over their home colony, their tiny bodies swaying to the beat of the world around them, they knew that they had achieved something truly special. They had proven that even the smallest among us can achieve greatness when we work together and move in harmony with the rhythm of life.

Their tiny feet tapped out a rhythm of gratitude as they looked up at the sky, grateful for the lessons they had learned and the victory they had achieved. And as they settled down to rest, their tiny bodies moving in perfect harmony, they knew that they would carry the rhythm of their journey with them always, a reminder of the power of working together and moving in harmony with the world around us.

# Chapter 12: The New Adventure

As the days passed, Alvin and his fellow ants settled back into their routine, tending to the needs of their colony and working together in perfect harmony. But despite the peace and order that had been restored to their home, Alvin couldn't help but feel a sense of restlessness. He longed for a new adventure, a new challenge to overcome.

One day, as he was out foraging for food, he came across a strange plant he had never seen before. Its leaves were a bright shade of purple, and it seemed to pulse with a faint, rhythmic energy.

Intrigued, Alvin took a closer look, and as he did, he felt a strange energy coursing through his tiny body. It was as though the plant was calling out to him, beckoning him to explore its secrets.

Without hesitation, Alvin gathered a team of his fellow ants, and together they set out on a new adventure, determined to uncover the mysteries of the strange plant.

As they journeyed deeper into the forest, their tiny feet tapping out a rhythm of excitement and anticipation, they encountered all manner of challenges, from treacherous terrain to fierce predators.

But with each challenge they faced, Alvin and his team drew on the lessons they had learned on their previous journey. They moved in perfect harmony, working together to overcome every obstacle in their path.

And as they drew closer to the plant, they could feel the rhythm of their journey intensifying, pulsing through their tiny bodies like a heartbeat.

Finally, they arrived at the plant, and as they began to explore its secrets, they were amazed by what they found. The plant was filled with a strange, pulsing energy, a rhythmic force that seemed to be alive.

With each passing moment, Alvin and his team felt themselves becoming more and more attuned to the rhythm of the plant, moving in perfect harmony with its pulsing energy.

And as they basked in the glow of the plant's rhythmic energy, they knew that they had uncovered something truly special, a new adventure that would guide them on a journey of discovery and growth for years to come.

Their tiny feet tapped out a rhythm of excitement and wonder as they looked up at the sky, grateful for the new adventure that lay ahead. And as they set off on their journey once again, they knew that they would carry the lessons of their previous journey with them always, moving in perfect harmony with the rhythm of life.

# Chapter 13: The Friendship

Alvin and his fellow ants had been on many adventures together, facing countless challenges and obstacles. But as they journeyed deeper into the forest, they began to realize that there was one thing that was more important than any adventure: friendship.

As they moved in perfect harmony, tapping out a rhythm of unity and trust, they began to understand the true power of friendship. They saw how it could help them overcome even the greatest obstacles, how it could inspire them to be their best selves, and how it could enrich their lives in ways they had never imagined.

And so, as they journeyed deeper into the forest, they made a pact to always be there for one another, to support each other through thick and thin, and to never forget the power of their friendship.

Together, they faced all manner of challenges, from treacherous terrain to fierce predators. But no matter what they encountered, they knew that they had each other's backs, and that they could overcome anything as long as they moved in perfect harmony.

And as they tapped out a rhythm of friendship, they felt a deep sense of gratitude for one another. They knew that their friendship was something special, something that would last a lifetime, and that no adventure could ever compare to the bond they had forged together.

As they reached the end of their journey, they looked back on all they had accomplished, all the challenges they had overcome, and all the memories they had made. And they knew that, no matter what adventures lay ahead, they would always move forward together, in perfect harmony, tapping out a rhythm of friendship that would guide them on their journey of life.

# Chapter 14: The Learning Journey

As the tiny ant Alvin and his friends continued on their adventures, they soon realized that every challenge they faced was an opportunity to learn and grow.

Whether it was navigating through the dark and dangerous tunnels of the ant colony or fighting off fierce predators in the forest, they saw each challenge as a chance to hone their skills and develop new ones.

They learned how to work together in perfect harmony, how to communicate effectively, and how to adapt to any situation. They also discovered that sometimes the greatest lessons came from their failures, when they were forced to reevaluate their approach and try new strategies.

As they journeyed on, tapping out their rhythm of unity and determination, they began to understand the true value of their experiences. They saw how each challenge had strengthened them, made them more resilient, and taught them something new about themselves and their fellow ants.

And as they looked back on their journey, they realized that they had grown in ways they never thought possible. They had become stronger, wiser, and more capable than they ever could have imagined.

But even as they celebrated their achievements, they knew that their learning journey was far from over. They still had much to discover, much to learn, and much to explore.

And so they tapped out a new rhythm, one of curiosity and wonder, as they set out on their next adventure, eager to see what new challenges and opportunities lay ahead. For they knew that every step of their journey, no matter how difficult or daunting, was a chance to learn, to grow, and to become the best ants they could be.

# Chapter 15: The Self-Discovery

As Alvin and his friends continued on their journey, they began to realize that there was more to life than just survival. They knew that they had a greater purpose, a reason for being that went beyond the daily grind of collecting food and building their colony.

And so, they began a new journey, one of self-discovery, as they searched for their true calling in life.

They explored the vast and wondrous world around them, tapping out a rhythm of curiosity and wonder as they discovered new plants, animals, and landscapes. They marveled at the beauty of the forest, the majesty of the mountains, and the mystery of the oceans.

But as they journeyed on, they also looked inward, exploring their own hearts and minds, and asking themselves what they truly wanted in life.

Some of them discovered a passion for music, tapping out intricate rhythms with their feet and antennae. Others found a love of storytelling, weaving intricate tales of adventure and heroism.

Still, others discovered a talent for leadership, guiding their fellow ants with wisdom and compassion. And some simply discovered the joy of being alive, of tapping out their own unique rhythm and dancing to the beat of their own heart.

As they embraced their true selves, they felt a sense of peace and fulfillment that they had never known before. They knew that they were living their lives to the fullest, tapping out a rhythm of self-discovery that would guide them on their journey of personal growth and fulfillment.

And as they journeyed on, they knew that their self-discovery journey was far from over. They still had much to explore, much to learn, and much to discover about themselves and the world around them.

But with each step they took, tapping out a rhythm of courage and self-assurance, they knew that they were on the right path, following their true calling and living their lives with purpose and passion.

# Chapter 16: The Problem-Solving

As Alvin and his friends continued their journey, they encountered many challenges and obstacles that threatened to derail their progress. But they refused to give up, tapping out a rhythm of determination and resilience as they faced each new problem head-on.

They quickly learned that problem-solving was an essential skill in life, and that by working together and using their unique talents and abilities, they could overcome even the toughest challenges.

One day, they encountered a massive boulder blocking their path. It was too heavy for any one ant to move, and they knew they needed to come up with a creative solution if they were going to continue on their journey.

Some of the ants used their strong jaws to chisel away at the rock, tapping out a rhythm of persistence and patience. Others used their keen senses to search for cracks and weaknesses in the rock, tapping out a rhythm of intuition and resourcefulness.

Together, they worked tirelessly, tapping out a rhythm of teamwork and collaboration, until finally, they managed to move the boulder out of their way and continue on their journey.

Another time, they encountered a raging river that seemed impossible to cross. But instead of giving up, they tapped out a rhythm of creativity and ingenuity, fashioning a raft out of leaves and sticks and using their own bodies to paddle across the river.

And so, as they journeyed on, they continued to face new problems and obstacles, but they always found a way to overcome them. They tapped out a rhythm of adaptability and flexibility, adjusting their plans and strategies as needed to stay on course and achieve their goals.

And as they mastered the art of problem-solving, they knew that they were becoming stronger, more resilient ants, ready to face whatever challenges lay ahead on their journey of life.

# Chapter 17: The Importance of Rest

As Alvin and his friends continued their long journey, they realized the importance of taking time to rest and recharge. They tapped out a rhythm of self-care and learned that taking care of themselves was just as important as taking care of their goals.

One day, Alvin noticed that some of his friends seemed tired and sluggish. They were having a hard time keeping up with the pace of their journey, and Alvin knew that they needed a break.

He suggested they take a short break and rest for a while, tapping out a rhythm of care and concern. His friends agreed, and they found a quiet spot to rest and recharge.

As they rested, Alvin and his friends tapped out a rhythm of gratitude, reflecting on all the progress they had made on their journey so far. They also tapped out a rhythm of reflection, thinking about their goals and the steps they needed to take to achieve them.

After their break, they felt refreshed and energized, tapping out a rhythm of renewed enthusiasm as they continued on their journey.

As they journeyed on, they made it a priority to take breaks and rest when they needed it. They tapped out a rhythm of self-awareness and learned to recognize when they needed to slow down and recharge.

They also discovered that taking time to rest and recharge actually made them more productive in the long run. They were able to tap out a rhythm of increased efficiency and focus, allowing them to achieve their goals more quickly and effectively.

And so, Alvin and his friends continued on their journey, tapping out a rhythm of balance and harmony between their goals and their need for rest and self-care. They knew that by taking care of themselves, they would be able to achieve even greater success in the long run.

# Chapter 18: The Homecoming

After many long weeks of travel, Alvin and his friends finally reached their destination - their home.

As they approached their familiar surroundings, they tapped out a rhythm of excitement and anticipation. They couldn't wait to be reunited with their families and share their incredible journey with them.

But as they got closer, they noticed that something was different. There was an eerie quietness in the air, and their homes looked empty and abandoned.

They tapped out a rhythm of confusion and worry, wondering what could have happened. They searched the area, calling out for their families, but there was no answer.

Finally, they found a note left behind by their loved ones. It explained that while they were away, a natural disaster had struck their town, and everyone had to evacuate.

Alvin and his friends tapped out a rhythm of shock and disbelief, unable to believe that their home was now gone. But they knew that they had to keep moving forward, and they tapped out a rhythm of determination to find a new home and start again.

They set out on a new journey, tapping out a rhythm of hope and perseverance. They traveled through different towns, meeting new friends along the way and searching for a place they could call home.

Finally, after many long months of searching, they found a new town that felt like home. They tapped out a rhythm of joy and relief, happy to have found a new place to start fresh.

And so, Alvin and his friends settled into their new home, tapping out a rhythm of gratitude for all the lessons they learned on their incredible journey. They knew that even though they faced many challenges along the way, their experiences had taught them the importance of resilience, friendship, and perseverance.

# Chapter 19: The Mystery of the Missing Ants

Alvin and his friends had settled into their new home and were enjoying their newfound sense of community. But one day, they noticed that some of their ant friends had gone missing.

Alvin tapped out a rhythm of concern and fear. He knew that something wasn't right, and he needed to get to the bottom of it.

He gathered his friends and set out to investigate the mystery of the missing ants. They tapped out a rhythm of determination as they searched high and low for any clues.

Finally, they came across a group of ants from a neighboring town. They seemed friendly at first, but as Alvin and his friends started to ask questions, they noticed that something was off.

The ants from the other town were evasive and defensive, refusing to answer any questions about the missing ants. Alvin and his friends tapped out a rhythm of suspicion and decided to keep a close eye on them.

One day, they followed the ants from the neighboring town and discovered a hidden lair deep in the woods. As they peered in, they saw their missing ant friends locked up in cages.

Alvin and his friends tapped out a rhythm of anger and sadness. They knew they had to act fast to rescue their friends and bring the culprits to justice.

They quickly formed a plan and executed it with precision. They tapped out a rhythm of bravery as they faced off against the evil ants from the neighboring town.

In the end, they were successful in rescuing their friends and putting a stop to the kidnappings. Alvin and his friends tapped out a rhythm of victory as they returned home, proud of their teamwork and perseverance.

And as they settled back into their daily rhythms, they knew that they could always count on each other to solve any mystery and overcome any obstacle.

# Chapter 20: The Unexpected Alliance

After the harrowing experience of the missing ants, Alvin and his friends were feeling grateful for each other and the sense of community they had built. But their peaceful life was about to be disrupted again.

One day, a group of unfamiliar ants showed up at their colony, asking for help. They were from a distant land and were being threatened by a common enemy – a group of ferocious beetles.

Alvin and his friends tapped out a rhythm of hesitation. They had never dealt with beetles before, and they were unsure if they should get involved. But as they heard the ants' story, they realized that the beetles were not just a threat to the newcomers but to all ant colonies.

They tapped out a rhythm of empathy and decided to form an unexpected alliance with the visiting ants. Together, they created a plan to defeat the beetles and protect all their homes.

The plan was risky, and they knew it would require everyone's cooperation and bravery. But they tapped out a rhythm of determination and set out to put the plan into action.

As they faced off against the beetles, Alvin and his friends tapped out a rhythm of unity, working closely with their new allies. They fought with everything they had, using their unique strengths to outsmart and overpower the beetles.

In the end, they emerged victorious. Alvin and his friends tapped out a rhythm of relief and pride. They had formed an unexpected alliance and had saved many lives.

As they said goodbye to their new friends, Alvin and his colony felt a sense of accomplishment and gratitude. They had learned that even when faced with unexpected challenges, they could rely on each other and form alliances to overcome any obstacle.

# Chapter 21: The Truth Revealed

Life in the ant colony had returned to normal, but Alvin couldn't shake the feeling that something wasn't right. He noticed that some ants had been acting strangely and avoiding him, and he couldn't figure out why.

One day, he overheard a group of ants whispering about a secret that they had been keeping from him. Alvin tapped out a rhythm of curiosity and approached them, demanding to know what was going on.

Reluctantly, the ants told him the truth – they had been stealing food from other colonies. They had convinced themselves that it was necessary to survive, but they knew it was wrong and had kept it hidden from Alvin and the rest of the colony.

Alvin was shocked and disappointed. He had always believed in fairness and honesty, and he couldn't believe that his fellow ants had betrayed those values. He tapped out a rhythm of disappointment and anger, unsure of what to do.

But after reflecting on the situation, Alvin tapped out a rhythm of forgiveness and decided to confront the ant thieves. He told them that what they were doing was wrong and that they needed to make amends for their actions.

Together, they came up with a plan to return the stolen food and apologize to the other colonies. It wasn't easy, and they faced some resistance and criticism from the other ants, but they tapped out a rhythm of determination and persisted.

In the end, they were able to make things right and restore their reputation in the ant community. Alvin and his friends tapped out a rhythm of relief and gratitude, knowing that they had learned an important lesson about the importance of honesty and accountability.

As they looked back on the experience, Alvin and his friends realized that sometimes the truth can be hard to confront, but it's always better to face it and take responsibility for your actions.

# Chapter 22: The Rebuilding

After the revelation about the ant thieves, the colony was left with a lot of work to do to rebuild their reputation and make amends with the other colonies. Alvin tapped out a rhythm of determination and started to organize a group of ants to help with the rebuilding effort.

They began by repairing any damage that had been done to the other colonies, offering assistance wherever they could. It was a slow process, but Alvin and his friends tapped out a rhythm of patience and perseverance, knowing that it would take time to earn back the trust of the other ants.

As they worked, they also reflected on what had led them down the path of stealing. They realized that they had been too focused on survival and had lost sight of their values. Alvin tapped out a rhythm of reflection and made a vow to himself and the rest of the colony that they would never lose sight of their values again.

The rebuilding effort wasn't just physical – it was also emotional. Alvin and his friends had to work to restore their relationships with the other ants, earning back their respect and trust. It wasn't easy, and there were times when it felt like they were taking one step forward and two steps back.

But they tapped out a rhythm of perseverance and kept at it, never giving up on their mission to make things right. Slowly but surely, they began to see progress – other colonies started to reach out to them for help, and they were welcomed back into the larger ant community.

As they looked back on their journey, Alvin and his friends realized that sometimes it takes a setback to remind you of what's truly important. They tapped out a rhythm of gratitude, knowing that they had learned a valuable lesson and had become better ants for it.

And as they settled back into their daily routine, they knew that they would never forget the importance of honesty, integrity, and the power of teamwork.

# Chapter 23: The Celebration

After months of hard work and dedication, the colony had finally earned back the trust and respect of the other ant colonies. To celebrate their success, Alvin and his friends organized a grand celebration to bring all the ant colonies together in one place.

Alvin tapped out a rhythm of joy and excitement as he helped to prepare for the festivities. The ants decorated the colony with bright flowers and ribbons, and everyone worked together to prepare a feast fit for a queen.

As the other colonies arrived, Alvin and his friends welcomed them with open arms, tapping out a rhythm of hospitality and warmth. They exchanged stories and shared food, dancing to the beat of the music that filled the air.

The celebration lasted well into the night, and everyone had a wonderful time. Alvin looked around at the happy faces of his fellow ants and tapped out a rhythm of contentment. It had been a long journey, but they had made it through together, stronger and more united than ever before.

As the night drew to a close, Alvin stood up and tapped out a rhythm of gratitude to the other ant colonies for their forgiveness and support. The other ants responded with a rhythm of their own, expressing their admiration for the hard work and determination that the colony had shown.

As Alvin and his friends settled back into their colony, they knew that they had made lifelong friends and allies in the other colonies. They tapped out a rhythm of peace and harmony, feeling grateful for the strong bonds that had been formed during their journey.

And as they drifted off to sleep, Alvin and his friends knew that they had accomplished something truly remarkable – they had not only rebuilt their colony, but they had also rebuilt their relationships with the other ants, creating a more united and stronger community than ever before.

# Chapter 24: The New Horizon

As the sun rose on a new day, Alvin stood at the edge of the colony, tapping out a rhythm of anticipation. He had heard whispers of a new land, far beyond the horizon, and he felt a pull towards the unknown.

Alvin knew that the journey would be long and filled with challenges, but he also knew that he was not alone. His friends stood beside him, tapping out a rhythm of courage and determination.

Together, they set out on a new adventure, leaving the safety of their colony behind. As they marched across the terrain, they encountered new obstacles and dangers, but Alvin and his friends tapped out a rhythm of perseverance and resilience, refusing to give up.

As they continued on their journey, they met new creatures and experienced new wonders, tapping out a rhythm of curiosity and wonder. They marveled at the beauty of the world around them and felt grateful for the opportunity to explore it.

As the days turned into weeks, and the weeks turned into months, Alvin and his friends grew stronger and more united than ever before. They tapped out a rhythm of camaraderie and trust, knowing that they could rely on each other no matter what.

Finally, after many months of travel, they reached their destination – a land filled with abundance and possibility. Alvin tapped out a rhythm of joy and excitement, knowing that this was the start of a new chapter in their journey.

As they settled into their new home, Alvin and his friends tapped out a rhythm of gratitude, thankful for all that they had experienced and all that was yet to come. They knew that they would face new challenges and obstacles, but they also knew that they were ready for anything that lay ahead.

And as they tapped out a rhythm of hope and optimism for the future, Alvin and his friends looked out at the horizon, eager for the next adventure to come.

# Chapter 25: The Great Migration

As the seasons changed and the weather grew colder, Alvin and his colony knew that it was time for the great migration. They tapped out a rhythm of preparation, gathering supplies and organizing themselves for the long journey ahead.

The journey would take them across mountains and through forests, over rivers and through valleys. But Alvin and his friends were ready, tapping out a rhythm of determination and endurance.

As they marched forward, they encountered new challenges and obstacles, but Alvin and his friends tapped out a rhythm of adaptability and creativity, finding new ways to overcome each obstacle in their path.

They passed by other colonies, exchanging greetings and sharing stories. They tapped out a rhythm of camaraderie and kinship, knowing that they were all in this together.

As they approached the end of their journey, Alvin and his friends tapped out a rhythm of excitement and anticipation. They could sense that they were nearing their new home, a place where they would settle for the winter months.

Finally, they reached their destination - a cozy underground nest, filled with warmth and comfort. Alvin and his friends tapped out a rhythm of relief and gratitude, thankful for their safe arrival and the opportunity to rest.

As the winter months passed by, Alvin and his colony thrived in their new home, tapping out a rhythm of contentment and satisfaction. And when spring arrived, they knew that it was time to begin the journey back to their original colony, tapping out a rhythm of readiness and excitement for the new adventure to come.

# Chapter 26: The Adaptation

As Alvin and his friends made their way back to their original colony, they realized that things had changed. The rhythm of life was different, and the familiar landscape had shifted.

Undeterred, Alvin and his friends tapped out a rhythm of curiosity and exploration, eager to discover what had happened in their absence.

They encountered new obstacles and challenges along the way, but Alvin and his friends tapped out a rhythm of flexibility and adaptability, finding new ways to navigate the changing terrain.

As they approached their old colony, Alvin and his friends sensed that something was wrong. The rhythm of life had been disrupted, and their fellow ants were struggling to adapt.

Alvin and his friends tapped out a rhythm of empathy and compassion, reaching out to their fellow ants and offering their support.

Together, they worked to find new solutions and strategies, tapping out a rhythm of collaboration and teamwork.

Slowly but surely, the colony began to adapt to the new challenges, tapping out a rhythm of resilience and determination.

And as the days turned into weeks, and the weeks turned into months, Alvin and his friends watched as the colony thrived once again, tapping out a rhythm of hope and optimism for the future.

# Chapter 28: The Community

Alvin had always known that ants were social creatures, but he didn't fully appreciate the power of community until he found himself leading his own colony.

As the leader, Alvin realized that it was up to him to set the tone and rhythm of the colony. He knew that if he wanted his colony to thrive, he needed to create a strong sense of community among his fellow ants.

Alvin and his friends tapped out a rhythm of inclusivity, welcoming new ants into their colony and making them feel at home.

They also tapped out a rhythm of cooperation, working together to achieve common goals and support one another through difficult times.

But perhaps most importantly, Alvin and his friends tapped out a rhythm of communication. They took the time to listen to each other's ideas and concerns, and they made sure that everyone's voice was heard.

Through their collective efforts, Alvin and his fellow ants built a strong and vibrant community, tapping out a rhythm of unity and belonging.

And as they went about their daily tasks, tapping out their own unique rhythms, Alvin knew that he was part of something truly special – a community that was greater than the sum of its parts.

# Chapter 29: The Natural Disaster

It had been a hot and dry summer, and Alvin and his colony were struggling to find enough food and water to survive. But just when things seemed like they couldn't get any worse, a natural disaster struck.

A sudden storm rolled in, bringing with it strong winds and heavy rain. The ants scrambled to protect their home and their food stores, but it was no use. The rain came down so hard that it flooded their colony and washed away their supplies.

Alvin and his friends were devastated. They had worked so hard to build up their colony, and now it was all gone. They didn't know how they were going to survive.

But as they huddled together, shivering in the rain, Alvin realized that they had one thing that the storm couldn't take away from them – their rhythm.

Despite the chaos and destruction around them, the ants continued to tap out their unique rhythms, keeping time with each other even as the world seemed to be falling apart.

And slowly but surely, they began to rebuild. They worked together to dig new tunnels and collect new food, tapping out a rhythm of resilience and determination.

And as they worked, Alvin realized that their rhythm wasn't just a way to communicate with each other – it was a way to connect with the natural world around them. Their rhythms were in sync with the ebb and flow of the rain, the wind, and the sun, reminding them that they were part of something much greater than themselves.

As the days and weeks passed, the colony emerged from the storm stronger and more resilient than ever before. And as they went about their daily tasks, tapping out their own unique rhythms, Alvin knew that they were ready for whatever challenges the natural world might throw their way.

# Chapter 30: The Homecoming, Again

As the tiny ant colony made their way through the dense jungle, they couldn't help but feel a sense of relief and excitement. They had been on a long journey, faced many obstacles, and had grown as a community in ways they never could have imagined. But now, as they approached their familiar hill, they realized something was different. The once lush and green forest had been replaced with scorched earth and charred trees. The colony was devastated to see their home destroyed by a recent wildfire.

As they regrouped and tried to come up with a plan, they heard a faint buzzing in the distance. It was a group of bees from a nearby hive, who had also been affected by the disaster. The two groups quickly formed an alliance, pooling their resources and working together to rebuild their homes and communities. With the help of the bees, the ants were able to rebuild their hill and create a new, stronger community. They learned that even in the face of adversity, they could rely on the support and cooperation of others to overcome challenges and thrive.

And as they settled into their new home, the ants couldn't help but feel a sense of gratitude for the journey that had led them there. They knew that the lessons they had learned and the bonds they had formed would stay with them for a lifetime, and they were excited to see what new adventures lay ahead.

# Epilogue:

As the sun began to set on the ant colony, the tiny creatures gathered around to listen to their leader's final words.

"Dear ants," the queen began, "we have been on an incredible journey together. We have faced challenges, overcome obstacles, and discovered the importance of working together as a team."

The ants nodded in agreement, their tiny heads bobbing up and down.

"But our journey doesn't end here. Our legacy will live on through our children and their children. We have taught them the importance of perseverance, of never giving up when faced with adversity."

The queen looked out over the colony, her heart swelling with pride. "We have created a community where every ant is valued, where every ant has a role to play. Let us continue to work together, to support each other, and to build a better future for our colony."

With those final words, the queen turned and walked away, leaving the ants to ponder the journey they had been on and the legacy they would leave behind. And as the stars twinkled in the sky above, the ants knew that their incredible journey was just beginning.

Printed in Great Britain
by Amazon

32161503R00030